THE BOOK OF

Fairies

NATURE SPIRITS
From Around the World

For T., M., S., E., and O., with my love—

R. W.

To Meaghan, Kristen, Erin and Jordie.

When you fly from the nest, may you realize all your dreams—

R. T. B.

Beyond Words Publishing, Inc.

20827 N.W. Cornell Road, Hillsboro, Oregon 97124

503-531-8700/1-800-284-9673

Graphic design by Design/Section

Printed in Hong Kong by South Sea International Press

Distributed to the book trade by Publishers Group West

Library of Congress Cataloging-in-Publication Data

Williams, Rose,
      The book of fairies : nature spirits from around the world /
retold by Rose Williams ; illustrated by Robin T. Barrett.
            p.   cm.
      Contents: The magic fountain (French) -- The star maiden (Ojibwa)
--The herb fairy (Chinese) -- The fairies' jewels (English) -- The
stone-cutter's wishes (Japanese) -- The mountain of the moon (Hindu)
-- The golden spear (Irish) -- How the fairies came (Algonquin).
      ISBN 1-885223-56-0
      1. Fairy tales. [1. Fairy tales. 2. Folklore.] I. Barrett,
Robin T., ill. II. Title.
PZ8.W66965Bo 1997
398.2--dc21   97-19943
                                                        CIP
                                                         AC

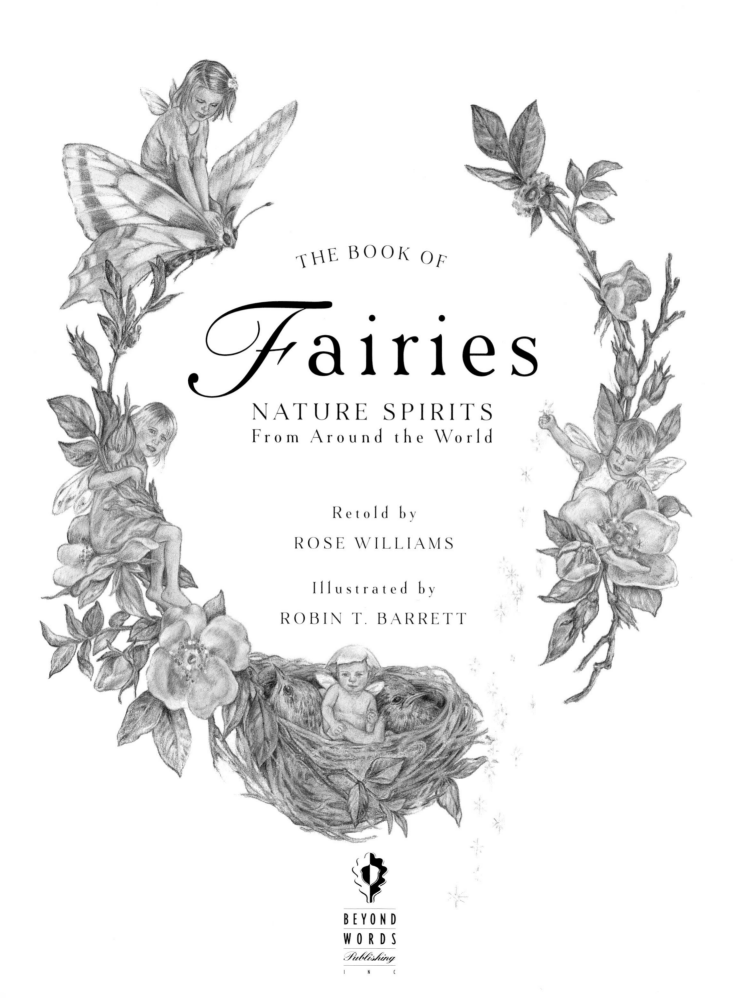

THE BOOK OF

Fairies

NATURE SPIRITS
From Around the World

Retold by

ROSE WILLIAMS

Illustrated by

ROBIN T. BARRETT

BEYOND
WORDS
Publishing
I N C

THE

Fairies

The fairies have never a penny to spend,

They haven't a thing put by,

But theirs is the dower of bird and of flower

And theirs are the earth and sky.

And though you should live in a palace of gold

Or sleep in a dried up ditch,

You could never be as poor as the fairies are,

And never as rich.

Since ever and ever the world began

They have danced like a ribbon of flame,

They have sung their song through the centuries long

And yet it is never the same.

And though you be foolish or though you be wise,

With hair of silver or gold,

You can never be as young as the fairies are,

And never as old.

Rose Fyleman

CONTENTS

Foreword

The fairy realm is a central aspect of cultures all over the world. As the title of this anthology indicates, there is a deep connection between fairies and nature. Many people acknowledge specific fairies as manifestations of the spiritual qualities of flowers and herbs, and associate larger spirits with rivers, trees and mountains.

In mythology, fairies or spirits often appear as agents between the world of human affairs and the invisible powers of the natural world. During our everyday lives, we witness changes in nature as the seasons pass, but those who live in very close contact with nature, as our ancestors did and as many traditional peoples continue to do, recognize that there is an inner as well as an outer aspect to these changes. Fairies are the characters in stories who illuminate the inner aspect — their activities often reveal the intimate connection between human beings and the world of nature.

Often fairies act in a healing capacity. They show humans which herbs and plants have the power to cure sickness of the body. In *The Herb Fairy*, from China, the Spirit of the Herbs shows a young woman how to find plants that will cure the local people of a terrible plague. Fairies also teach us which aspects of the human heart to value. In *The Magic Fountain*, from France, the Fairy of the Meadows shows two young people the importance of keeping promises; the Spirit of the Mountain in *The Stone-cutter's Wishes*, from Japan, teaches a stone-cutter that no power is limitless so that he learns

to appreciate an apparently simple life; and in the Algonquin story, *How the Fairies Came*, a mysterious stranger teaches the value of humility.

The power of fairies is usually greater than that of mortals, as the above stories show. This superior power is also apparent in the English tale, *The Fairies' Jewels*, in which a beautiful princess depends on the help of the fairies in preparing for her marriage; and in *The Golden Spear*, from Ireland, it is the fairies who lead two ordinary but good-hearted children towards great destinies. However, in spite of this power, fairies are sometimes vulnerable to foolish and rash behavior themselves. So, in *The Mountain of the Moon*, from India, two ice fairies get into trouble when, against their own accepted wisdom, they stray down from the wilderness of the Himalayas into human territory. There are also situations in which fairies rely on human assistance – in *The Star Maiden*, from the Ojibwa of North America, a star fairy depends on her contact with a mortal to find an earthly home for herself.

So as well as being exciting adventures, the stories in this collection show some of the ways in which fairies reveal to humans the secrets and laws of the natural world. The *Fairy Flora* section at the end of the book describes flowers, herbs and trees that have a particular connection with fairies and explains the customs and legends surrounding them. I hope that you will enjoy *The Book of Fairies* and that reading this anthology will bring you a little closer to the fairy realm that is around you in your own life.

Rose Williams 1997

Magic Fountain

In a small village deep in the countryside of France there once lived two children. The boy was called Sylvain. He was tall and handsome, with dark hair and deep-brown eyes. The girl was called Jocosa. She was slim and pretty, with blue eyes and curly blonde hair. The two children had been friends all their lives. Every day they looked after their flocks of sheep, and sat in the shade of a hawthorn bush, talking together.

One day the Fairy of the Meadows saw the two children, sitting among the sheep. Jocosa was listening to Sylvain who was playing a pipe he had made from reeds. "What lovely children," she thought, "and they are so fond of each other. I will take them under my special protection and keep them from harm."

She decided she would leave small gifts of cakes or sweets where she knew the children would find them. If Sylvain found the food, he would immediately offer some to Jocosa. If Jocosa saw the food first, she would call out to Sylvain, "Look at this cake lying under the hawthorn bush. I'll cut a piece for you."

The years passed by and the children grew into two young people who cared for each

9

other more than for anyone else in the world. One fine spring morning, the Fairy of the Meadows decided it was time to show herself to them. Walking quietly across the grass, she stood in front of Sylvain and Jocosa. They leapt to their feet and stared in astonishment at the beautiful fairy, dressed all in green and wearing a crown of wild flowers on her head.

"Don't be afraid," the fairy said, "I am the Fairy of the Meadows and for many years I have protected you. I was the person who left you those gifts to find and enjoy. Now it is time for you to do something for me in return."

Sylvain bowed his head because he realized the Fairy was a queen in her own land. "Of course," he replied quickly, and Jocosa nodded in agreement.

"You know that little fountain which bubbles up where the stream leaves the meadow and runs into the woods? I want you to promise me that each morning at sunrise you will go there and clear away any leaves or twigs which have fallen on it. If you do this every day, you will never be parted."

Sylvain and Jocosa happily gave their promise. Each morning they met at the fountain where they cleared away all the leaves and twigs. The fountain, with its clear water sparkling in the sunlight, became the prettiest in the whole countryside. They kept their promise to the fairy for many months. But early one summer's morning, as the two hurried towards the fountain, they both noticed bright clusters of beautiful poppies and buttercups and forget-me-nots growing thickly in the field.

"I'll take a bunch to Sylvain," thought Jocosa.

"I'll make a garland for Jocosa," decided Sylvain.

They were so busy picking the flowers that they did not notice the sun rising above the horizon. Suddenly the first bright rays of light shone across the country and they both realized that they would be too late to tidy the fountain. Dropping their flowers in dismay, they ran towards it. As each stood on either side of the bank, they saw that the waters were already muddied and seething. The little stream had become a river, swollen by torrents of water which flowed and rushed between them.

"Wait for me, Jocosa!" cried Sylvain. Desperately he jumped into the waters and tried to swim across, but in vain. The current was too strong and drove him back to the bank.

"I'll come to you!" called Jocosa. She tried to throw some branches over the water to make a bridge, but the current swept them away.

"Let's follow the river," Sylvain shouted across to Jocosa, "until we find a bridge or a boat further along."

So they started walking along each bank, but the river grew wider and wider until they could hardly see each other. Because they could not bear to be separated, they struggled on day and night, over mountains and through valleys, in the heat of summer and the cold of winter.

For three years they kept walking, always hoping that one day they would be together again. Finally they found themselves standing on towering cliffs where the river surged into the sea. They looked at each other across the great distance and despaired because they were further away from each other than ever. At this moment the Fairy of the Meadows, who

11

had kept them safe on their long journeys, decided they had suffered enough. She used her magic powers and in an instant they found themselves on the golden sands.

"Oh Jocosa!" Sylvain cried out joyfully, and they ran to hug each other.

Then Jocosa said, "We are to blame for our suffering because we did not keep our promise to the Fairy of the Meadows."

"Yes," Sylvain agreed sadly. "It was all our fault."

When the Fairy heard how sorry they were, she appeared in front of them. Jocosa and Sylvian begged her to forgive them. She smiled and touched them lightly on their shoulders.

"Don't be unhappy anymore," she said, "for now it is time for you to return to your home." Using her magic powers once more, the Fairy whisked Sylvain and Jocosa through the air. The next moment they were standing beside their precious fountain, which once more sparkled pure and clear. Their parents gladly agreed to the marriage of their children. A little cottage was prepared for them near to the magic fountain. The wedding day was arranged and the Fairy of the Meadows was to be the guest of honor. Before the wedding,

while they were waiting for the other guests to arrive, the Fairy of the Meadows called Sylvain and Jocosa to her. The three of them sat down in the rose-covered porch of the cottage and the Fairy said, "I want you to listen to this story which I am now going to tell you."

"Once upon a time, there was a greedy Sultan. He neglected his people and yearned for things he could not have. Although his palace was the finest in the land, the Sultan longed for more riches. The fairies and spirits, who saw the suffering of his people, decided to teach him a lesson. One of the fairies disguised herself as a beautiful golden bird and flew to the palace gardens. There, a servant caught the bird and offered it to the Sultan. The Sultan took the beautiful bird into his hands and admired the gleam of its wings. He noticed that under one wing were the words, 'He who eats my head will rule a land,' and under the other wing the words, 'He who eats my heart will find a hundred gold pieces under his pillow every morning.' The Sultan gave the bird back to the servant.

'Get your wife to cook this bird at once,' he ordered. 'Let me know when the food is ready. And don't tell anyone about this.'

"The servant ran home to his wife and, in spite of the Sultan's orders, he told her about the strange words written under the wings of the golden bird. The wife immediately made a stew out of the bird and decided to feed the head and heart to her own children so they would be rich and powerful. But as soon as the bird went into the pot, the fairy disguised within it slipped away and she flew back to her own land. There, everyone waited to see what would happen next.

"Meantime, the impatient Sultan came storming into the servant's home.

"'Give me that stew!' he demanded and, grabbing the dish, he began looking for the head and the heart of the golden bird! When he found that these two parts were missing, he thought the servant and his wife had eaten the pieces themselves. In a terrible fury, he vowed to punish the whole family before sundown.

"As soon as the Sultan had left, the wife told her husband what she had done. The couple decided that they must send their sons away immediately to escape the Sultan's anger. They embraced the two boys and sent them off into the world to seek their fortunes.

"The younger brother, who had eaten the heart of the golden bird, discovered that the words under its wing were quite true. Every morning he found a hundred gold pieces under his pillow. But instead of doing good for others with all this money, he spent it all on himself. People soon learned of his great wealth, and one day he was attacked and killed by robbers who then stole his hoard of gold.

"The elder brother, who had eaten the bird's head, also found out that the words under its wing were true. He traveled far and wide until he reached a mighty city in Asia. It happened that the people of this city were choosing a new Emir to rule over them, but disagreed over who would be the best man. While they were squabbling, the elder brother strode into the city. As he walked, a snow-white pigeon flew down from the city walls and settled on his head.

"Someone in the crowd cried out, 'It's an omen! It's an omen! He must be the new Emir!'

"Everybody agreed that the young man should be their new ruler. And so it was. The elder brother was declared Emir, but he knew nothing about governing people and he grew

14

cruel with his new powers. He treated his subjects very badly and became a tyrant. Eventually his people rebelled and killed him."

"And so," finished the Fairy of the Meadows, "you see how wealth and power did not bring happiness to the Sultan or the two brothers. You will lack for nothing if you lead a contented life and do not seek riches and power of which you have no need. If you always keep your promises and live happily together in this little cottage, I will watch over and protect you from harm."

Sylvain and Jocosa readily gave their promise, for they remembered what had happened to them when they broke their promise as children. Their families and friends gathered for their wedding, and afterwards the young couple lived in peace and great contentment in their little cottage by the magic fountain. The Fairy of the Meadows also kept her promise. With her protection, Sylvain and Jocosa lived for many years.

16

Star Maiden

O J I B W A

There are some countries which are especially loved by the fairy world. Often these are lands with great forests, deep lakes and grassy meadows, where fairies live quietly and in harmony with the local people. One such land is the home of the Ojibwa, a proud and fearless nation which once lived freely in the continent that is now North America. In the wild parts of this land, the fairies made their winter homes in the roots and hollows of the old trees. In springtime they came out to live among the sweetly scented blossoms which clustered thickly on fruit trees and bushes. In autumn the fairies sheltered among the mushrooms that grew in the safe parts of the valleys and forests.

The Ojibwa knew all about the fairies who lived among them. They enjoyed the special friendship which sometimes flourishes between the human and the spirit world, and they were careful not to destroy the secret places where the fairies lived. At the end of the day when their work was done, the people would sit quietly in the entrances of their homes and rest. They would watch the smoke of their pipes curling up into the still air, listening in silence to the voices of the fairies. The fairies' voices were little more than whispers or hums,

rather like the sound of honey-bees, which even the youngest Ojibwa children could recognize. One evening, a clan of Ojibwa was gathered as usual near their campfire. Everyone was listening to the tiny noises of the night when one of the young braves saw something which made his eyes grow wide. Silently he rose to his feet. The others turned to see what he was looking at. Then they, too, stood up in wonder. Just beyond the glow of the fire stood several tall trees and in the very top of the tallest tree they could see a bright, shining light. What could possibly be making this glittering light? Without a sound they all moved towards the trees to have a closer look.

At the foot of the tallest tree, the people stopped and gazed upwards. The young brave with the sharp eyes knew at once what was shining so brightly. "It's a great star," he told the other warriors, "It's caught in the top branches of the tree."

The wise chiefs were quickly summoned and they all gathered for a pow-wow. For three nights they sat in council trying to decide what to do about the beautiful star which was trapped in the tree top. At the end of the third night, they still did not know why the star had come to earth or how to help it. Then, on the fourth night, the young brave who had first seen the star came before the council. He explained that he had learned the truth about the star while he had been sleeping.

"As I lay asleep," he said, "the West Wind lifted the curtain of my wigwam. The light from the star fell in a radiant beam across the ground near where I lay. It was so brilliant that I could hardly look at it. Then I saw a beautiful girl, lovelier by far than any human woman. I was struck dumb with astonishment. The girl spoke to me and her voice was like the

18

voice of the birds at sunrise. She told me that she was the Star Maiden and her home was in the star. Then she told me how together she and the star had wandered in the skies above the earth, and she had seen many beautiful countries but none so fair as this land of ours.

'If you would allow me,' she said, 'I would like to live among you and wander no longer above the earth. If you were to let me stay, the star would be released to return to the heavens and I would make my home with your people for ever.' Before I could reply she dissolved into the light around her. Then the beam of light disappeared, the curtain of my wigwam closed, and everything was quiet once more."

When the council of elders heard this, they were very pleased and honored. They told the young brave that if the Star Maiden returned to him the following evening, he was to invite her to choose any place among their prairies and mountains and lakes in which to make her home. And so it happened. That night, the Star Maiden came again to the young brave's wigwam and he gave her the elders' message.

At once the Star Maiden started to search for the best place to make her home. On the vast prairies which stretched to the horizons, she found beautiful prairie flowers growing. Close to these flowers was a ring of mushrooms, and the Star Maiden hoped that earthly fairies would gather here on moonlit nights. "I shall rest here until the fairies come," she thought, "and then make a home among them." So she perched on one of the mushrooms waiting for the night. But the fairies never came and the star did not move — it still lay trapped in the top of the tall tree. Then, the Star Maiden heard a terrible, thundering sound that shook the earth. In great fear, she fled from the mushroom just as a huge herd of buffalo charged across the prairie. This was no place for the Star Maiden to make her home!

Leaving the plains behind her, the Star Maiden next tried the mountains. Here, she found fragrant wild rose bushes hugging the soft, moss-covered slopes. There was a wonderful, peaceful silence.

"This is where I shall live," thought the Star Maiden. "There are no buffalo herds and from these mountain tops I can see my friends among the stars." So she settled down inside a perfect wild rose. But, again, the star did not move — it still lay trapped in the top of the tall tree.

Before many days had passed, the Star Maiden found that she was not happy. The mountains were steep and great rocks towered round her resting place. "I cannot see the people of this beautiful land," she thought. "They live in the valleys and I cannot see them from the mountain top."

So once again the Star Maiden set off to find a home. She flew back towards the valley where her star lay trapped and where the Ojibwa wigwams stood. Soon she came to the lake and looked around to see if there was any place for her to settle. In the middle of the water she noticed a gleaming white flower with a golden center, which shone in the warm sunlight. The flower was a water lily floating on the still surface of the lake. As the Star Maiden gazed at this beautiful plant, she saw a canoe glide across the water close to where the water lily was growing. Then she saw that the canoe was steered by the brave who had first discovered her star in the tree top.

"This will be my home," she announced happily, and she flew across the water to the great golden heart of the water lily. As she settled inside it, the star lifted free from the treetop and spun away into the sky. That night, the Star Maiden saw the stars reflected in the waters of the lake. "From here I can still see my star friends," she thought contentedly.

The next morning she saw that many of the Ojibwa children were playing on the edge of the water while the young braves canoed on the lake. "This is the best place to be," the Star Maiden decided. "Here I am safe from buffalo, here I can see the stars, and here I am among my new friends." So she made her home in the creamy petals of the water lily. And if you sit quietly at the shores of a lake where water lilies grow, you may be lucky enough to see or hear her — for the Ojibwa say that she lives there still, and that her song is like the voice of the birds at sunrise.

THE
Herb Fairy
CHINESE

In a distant part of China there once lived a great lord whose name was Wu Ming`. He was very rich, very strong and very cruel. His wife and his favorite courtiers dressed in rich silks and fine brocades. They threaded gold and silver flowers into their hair and wore rich gemstones on their fingers. But the poor peasants of the land slaved at their work. Wu Ming seized everything they earned. If anyone tried to resist, he threw the offender into prison.

Living in Wu Ming's magnificent palace was a girl called Chun Tao``. She was more beautiful than the lovely peach blossom after which she was named. She could embroider the most exquisite flowers and birds, but her special talent was her knowledge of herbs. Her job was to prepare medicines for the household because she knew more about herbs than anyone else. She would heal the sick with her soothing touch and gentle voice. While the courtiers at the palace dined on plates of gold in a hall hung with silver brocade, Chun Tao preferred to run beyond the palace gardens into the wilderness nearby. Here she ate wild berries, drank from the streams and studied the herbs and plants which grew thickly in the woods. Although many people in the palace feared their lord, Chun Tao did not.

` *Wu Ming (Woo Ming) means No Light.*

`` *Chun Tao (Choon Dao) means peach blossom, a symbol of immortality.*

She wandered wherever she chose, with garlands of freshly picked wild flowers crowning her sleek, dark hair.

The peasants who lived near the palace loved Chun Tao. She would always find time to speak to them and help them when they were sick. Because she knew which herbs made the best medicines, she saved many sick children. Although the palace sorcerer was supposed to be the most powerful magician in the land, many people believed that Chun Tao's gift was greater. But Chun Tao knew otherwise. The sorcerer was the only person who made her tremble, for she knew that he was jealous of her and wanted to destroy her. She also knew that his magic was evil.

Then one year, a terrible plague struck the land. Many people, rich and poor, young and old, became ill and died. Wu Ming and his advisers made a plan to save the courtiers of the palace. The gates were locked and a great ditch dug outside the walls so that no one could enter. Soldiers marched round the top of the wall to stop anyone getting inside. Wu Ming did not care about the peasants. It did not matter to him if they died of the plague as long as he was safe.

Chun Tao stood near the locked gates and wondered what she could do to help the poor people outside the walls. She could not get through the gates and she could not climb over the walls. Suddenly, she had an idea. She found an old wooden tub lying in the kitchens and she carried it into the gardens. Then she filled the tub with armfuls of peach blossoms from the gardens, pulled it to the stream which ran through the palace grounds and quickly hid herself beneath the flowers.

The tub spun slowly round in the stream and gradually began to move faster as it was caught up in the flowing water. The stream ran underneath the palace wall and it joined a river which flowed across the great open plains. Chun Tao, hidden in the tub, was carried safely along until the river passed the slopes of Miracle Mountain. Here the tub stuck fast on the river bank and Chun Tao climbed out.

All around on the side of the mountain grew every kind of herb and plant. Chun Tao knew these would help the poor peasants caught by the plague. She gathered them quickly and carefully, until her hands were almost full. Suddenly she froze in fear. Above her, swooping down from the sky, was a great white heron. Its claws stretched out to land on a

mountain crag, and as soon as they touched the rock, the heron turned into a white stag.
The stag sprang down the mountainside. Then, as its hooves touched the mountainside, it
turned instantly into a young man. The young man was as tall and slender as the mountain
saplings. His eyes shone like stars as he and Chun Tao stared at each other.

"Why are you gathering herbs?" the young man asked Chun Tao.

"Because I know about the healing power of herbs," she replied. "I want to help the poor
people who are ill and suffering from the plague."

At her answer the young man smiled. "I knew you were special when I first saw you,"
he said. "I am the Spirit of the Herbs and I can show you where the best herbs grow. Come
with me!"

Hand in hand, they climbed up Miracle Mountain, through the clouds which were gathered round its top. At last they came to the home of the Spirit of the Herbs, right at the top of the mountain. Chun Tao gazed round in awe. In front of her were the best and most precious herbs, all growing together in a vast, sun-drenched field.

Chun Tao ran to collect some. She knew that she needed to go at once to help the sick people. She smiled shyly at the young man and was sad that she had to leave him. The Spirit of the Herbs held out a small blue flower.

"I know you must go now to help the people with your skill, but when you wish to return to me, eat this blue flower. It will help you find me." So Chun Tao hid the blue flower safely in the folds of her skirt and hurried away.

Meanwhile at the palace, Wu Ming had discovered that Chun Tao was missing. Worse still, he was not feeling at all well. "Where are my medicines?" he demanded.

"Where is my servant girl?" he shouted. Then he ordered all the soldiers and all the servants to search for Chun Tao.

After seven days some of his soldiers returned to the palace. They had a strange story to tell. "Master," they said, "we have heard that the plague is over, the sick are recovering and it is the girl, Chun Tao, who has done this."

In a fury, Wu Ming threw the soldiers into prison and ordered that his fastest horse be harnessed. Then he rode out into the countryside with his courtiers and soldiers, determined to find Chun Tao. At the side of the plain where Miracle Mountain rose, he heard some news. The peasants there said that a young girl, after she had cured everyone of the plague, had eaten a small blue flower, turned into a white heron and flown away up the mountain side. Furious that Chun Tao had escaped him, Wu Ming galloped back to his palace and summoned his sorcerer, ordering him to find her.

At the top of Miracle Mountain, Chun Tao and the Spirit of the Herbs lived happily together, unaware of the evil plot Wu Ming and his sorcerer were making. They lived in contentment until summer was over and the cold winter arrived. The birds hid in their nests

27

and the animals retreated to their burrows and holes. Because he was from the fairy kingdom, the Spirit of the Herbs did not feel the cold, but poor Chun Tao suffered terribly from the icy wind. Before long, her husband decided that he must go down to the land of the humans to find a warm cloak for his poor bride.

As the Spirit of the Herbs approached the palace, he met the sorcerer at the gates. The sorcerer was carrying a beautiful magic cloak over his arm and the Spirit of the Herbs stopped him.

"Will you give me your cloak?" he asked the sorcerer. "I need it for my wife who is suffering terribly from this cold."

"Yes," replied the wicked sorcerer with a cruel smile. "I would like to help you. I will give it to you as a present for your wife. It is a magic cloak and feels softer than feathers and lighter than down."

After thanking the sorcerer, the Spirit of the Herbs flew quickly back to Chun Tao and told her how he had been given the cloak by the sorcerer.

Chun Tao shook her head. "I am afraid of this cloak," she said. "The sorcerer means us harm." But the Spirit of the Herbs did not believe her. To show her how warm and safe the cloak was, he smiled and wrapped it round his own shoulders.

In an instant there was a great roar in the mountains and one side of Miracle Mountain split open from the summit to the bottom, forming a mighty gorge. In the same moment the Spirit of the Herbs was turned by the sorcerer's magic cloak into a shell which fell over the side of the mountain into the new gorge.

Chun Tao gave a cry of despair and stretched out her hands, trying to catch the falling shell – but in vain. Her hands clutched at the cold air and she leaned, frantic, over the edge of the abyss. Her voice echoed down the mountainside to where the beautiful shell was resting in the water at the bottom.

The Spirit of the Herbs called back up to Chun Tao. "Do not grieve. My friends will help you. The Spirit of the Mountain will protect you and all the herbs and plants will serve you. Each spring, before the flowers are in bud, the Spirit of the Wind will carry me back to

you and for three months I shall be restored to my former self. Please go on helping people. Take care of the poor people and tend to the herbs just as we did when we were together."

Chun Tao dried her eyes and agreed to do as the Spirit of the Herbs had asked her. But first she was determined to punish Wu Ming. She walked boldly back to the palace, and everybody wondered why she had returned. Wu Ming thought she had come back because she was afraid of him. He summoned her to his throne room. "You are my slave!" he thundered. "Your first duty is to serve and obey me!"

Chun Tao looked at Wu Ming in silence. Then she held out a strange-looking herb and said softly, "However powerful you may be, you cannot change the course of my life, or of yours. It is true that I have returned, but now I am a free person and I will not be your slave. Here! This is the only thing that I can do for you. Taste this plant. It is said that those who eat it will never argue again. No one will go against their spoken orders, no one will disobey their commands."

The vain Wu Ming was delighted, and without a moment's thought, he ate the herb. Immediately his tongue began to burn. He tried to cry out – but no sound came. He had been struck dumb. He could no longer shout orders at his terrified servants – and he remained silent for the rest of his life.

No one ever saw Chun Tao again, although some say they spotted a white heron flying towards Miracle Mountain when she disappeared. Although few people are aware of it, Chun Tao became the Herb Fairy. Ever since that day, she has tended the plants in place of her beloved Spirit of the Herbs. Her husband is always in her thoughts, and each spring the Spirit of the Wind carries him back to join her for three months among the herbs and flowers on Miracle Mountain.

THE

Fairies' Jewels

ENGLISH

Long, long ago in a faraway city, close to the
crystal mountains, there lived a beautiful princess
whose name was Crystalbelle. Her face was as pale and as lovely as a lily. Her eyes were as
dark as the sea. Her raven-black hair was long and hung round her shoulders in dark shiny
curls. The princess was not only very beautiful but was also good and kind. She cared for
the people of her land. If she heard of a family troubled by sickness or poverty, she would
call one of her courtiers.

"Please help this family," she would command, and the courtier would visit the family to
offer food and medicines.

All the people, as well as the courtiers in the palace, loved the princess for her beauty
and her goodness. The princess had many, many friends among her own people but she had
also made friends with the fairies.

The fairies of the crystal mountains had grown to love Princess Crystalbelle more than
any other human person. They would search in the secret valleys and they would search in
the secret forests, looking for something special to show the princess. Princess Crystalbelle

33

loved surprises, and the fairies would bring her little gifts. But they had to search for something unusual because the princess already had almost everything in the world.

"Do you think Princess Crystalbelle would like to see this rare butterfly?" the fairies asked each other. And the princess clapped her hands in delight at the beautiful colors on the butterfly's wings. When the fairies set the butterfly free, the princess gazed after it as it fluttered away over the palace gardens.

"Do you think Princess Crystalbelle would like to taste these luscious, ripe fruits?" the fairies wondered. And when the princess bit into the sweet, juicy fruits, she laughed with pleasure, and then offered some to her ladies-in-waiting.

"Do you think Princess Crystalbelle would like to listen to this rare bird's song?" the fairies said to one another. And the princess sat in silence, entranced by the pure notes sung by the bird. "Its singing is more beautiful than the music played by the palace musicians," the princess declared. The fairies taught her how to tame the bird, and each morning it flew to her window and woke her with its song.

One day the princess called all the fairies together. She had some exciting news to tell them and she wanted them to know before anyone else in the land.

"I am soon to be married," she told the fairies. "I am going to marry the Prince of the Far Isles Over the Sea. My wedding dress will be made from the soft white light of moonbeams. It will be trimmed with the pink clouds of the dawn. On my feet will be little slippers fashioned from the twinkling stars."

The fairies were thrilled and knew that Crystalbelle's wedding would be the grandest ever seen. One fairy spoke up, "But what shall you wear in your hair, Crystalbelle? You have nothing." The fairies looked at the princess and they looked at each other. What would be beautiful enough for Princess Crystalbelle to wear in her hair on her wedding day?

"I know," cried one fairy, "you must wear flowers!"

"Yes, yes!" exclaimed Princess Crystalbelle. "Of course. Flowers will be perfect for my hair on my wedding day!"

So all the fairies flew off in different directions to gather flowers. Some collected roses, pink and red, white and yellow. Others picked wild lilies, as pale and as beautiful as the princess herself. Others found sprays and trailing stems of jasmine with its rich, heavy scent. Back they flew to the palace with their arms filled with the most beautiful and fragrant blossoms, and they laid the flowers in great heaps at the feet of the princess.

"Wear my roses," said one fairy. "See how they glow in your hair!"

"Wear my lilies," cried another fairy. "See how they reflect your lovely face!"

"Wear my jasmine," called a third. "See how they wrap you in a cloud of fragrance!"

"Oh dear! Oh dear!" sighed Princess Crystalbelle, holding up the roses, and the lilies and the jasmine, trying to make up her mind. All the blossoms looked wonderful in her thick black tresses, and she found it very difficult to decide. It was true the roses glowed in her hair. It was true that her own face was as beautiful as the lilies. It was true that the jasmine

wrapped her in a cloud of fragrance. In the end the fairies argued so long about which were the most beautiful that the flowers wilted and died.

The fairies looked at the princess and they looked at each other.

"Oh dear! Oh dear! What shall I do?" cried the princess.

"This won't do," said the fairies. "We must find something which will not die as the flowers have died." They all sat round the princess, trying to think of something for her to wear in her hair on her wedding day, but no one had any ideas. Then, just as everyone began to despair, three fairies all looked up at the same moment and smiled at each other.

"Yes, we know," the three fairies said together and away they flew, over the palace gardens and towards the top of the crystal mountains. They flew through the sparkling air and finally landed where the crystal gleamed purest of all. Then each one looked around carefully. When they had all agreed which was the best, the most brilliant, the most sparkling piece of crystal, each fairy chipped off a little piece of rock. Holding the pieces safely in their hands, they nodded at each other.

"I know a mermaid who will help!" cried the first fairy.

"My friends the pixies will know what to do!" said the second fairy.

"I shall ask my friends the fire-gnomes!" declared the third fairy, and they all flew off in different directions.

The first fairy took her piece of rock down to the sea shore. On the edge of the sea, in a deep underwater cave which was washed by the tides, lived the mermaid who was a good friend of the fairy.

"Mermaid, mermaid!" the fairy called as she flew onto the sand. And the mermaid swam up through the blue waters and rested on a rock near where the fairy stood.

"Here is a piece of rock from the top of the crystal mountains," said the fairy. "Please take it for me and dip it in the depths of the deepest part of the sea."

So the mermaid took the rock and dove into the depths of the deepest part of the sea. Down she swam, down past the rocks and caves, down past the shoals of fish and the sea monsters, down and down through the blue waters. Now the mermaid knew and the fairy

knew that anything dipped into the depths of the deepest part of the sea would be changed.
It would take on part of the sea itself and be changed forever. When the mermaid returned
to the fairy waiting on the sands, she held up the crystal.

"Look!" cried the mermaid, and they both saw at once that the crystal had changed.
Now it was a deep blue color like the sea, shining and glowing in the sunlight.

It was the first sapphire.

Meanwhile the second fairy had flown with her piece of rock to the edge of the great
green forest. In this forest, among the roots and hollows of the trees, lived the pixies who
were friends of the fairy.

"Pixies, pixies!" called out the fairy. And the pixies peeped out from the deep green of
the undergrowth and ran to the fairy.

"Here is a piece of rock from the top of the crystal mountains," said the fairy. "Please

take it for me and hide it in the depths of the deepest part of the forest."

So the pixies took the rock into the depths of the deepest part of the forest. Along the hidden green paths, through the dense thickets and tangled branches, through to the green heart of the forest. Now the pixies and the fairy knew that anything hidden in the depths of the deepest part of the forest would be changed. It would take on part of the forest itself and be changed forever. When the pixies returned to the waiting fairy, they held up the crystal.

"Look!" cried the pixies, and everyone saw at once that the crystal had changed. Now it was a deep green color like the trees of the forest, shining and glowing in the sunlight.

It was the first emerald.

When the third fairy left the top of the crystal mountains, she flew with her piece of rock to another mountain. In the side of this mountain, hidden among hundreds of tunnels and caves, lived the fire-gnomes who were friends of the fairy.

"Gnomes, gnomes!" called out the fairy. And the fire-gnomes scuttled along their deep tunnels and peered out at her.

"Here is a piece of rock from the top of the crystal mountains," said the fairy. "Please take it for me down to the depths of the deepest part of your mountain."

So the fire-gnomes took the rock into the depths of the deepest part of their mountain. Along the darkest tunnels, down the steepest shafts, through to the fires burning in the center of the mountain. Now the gnomes knew and the fairy knew that anything hidden in the depths of the deepest part of the mountain would be changed by the fires burning there. It would take on part of the fire itself and be changed forever. When the gnomes returned to the waiting fairy, they held up the crystal.

"Look!" cried the gnomes, and everyone saw at once that the crystal had changed. Now it was a deep red color like the heart of the fire, shining and glowing in the sunlight.

It was the first ruby.

The three fairies flew back to Princess Crystalbelle. They laid all their beautiful gems at her feet, and everybody saw the wonderful colors as the jewels shimmered in the sunlight.

The princess clapped her hands. "How lovely they are!" she exclaimed. "That one looks like the blue of the sea, and that one is as green as the forest and the red one gleams like the heart of a fire."

The fairies held up each jewel in turn and each one flashed and shone against Crystalbelle's lovely hair. "I cannot decide," said the Princess after she had looked in her mirror a hundred times. So in the end, the Princess said she would wear all three jewels together and the fairies held them up against her beautiful hair for her to see.

The princess turned her head from side to side and gazed at her reflection in the mirror. "Oh dear! Oh dear!" cried the fairies. They didn't like the three jewels together. "What shall we do? What can Princess Crystalbelle wear in her hair on her wedding day?"

All the fairies looked at each other in dismay. No one could think of anything more

beautiful than the sapphire, the emerald and the ruby. All this time, a very small elf
had been sitting quietly in a corner, saying nothing but thinking hard. Now he came
forward and stood before the princess.

"Give me the jewels," he said. "I know what to do." And he gathered up the stones and

flew away, above the top of the palace and the top of the crystal mountains, up through the
circling clouds and misty sunshine.

"Sun-fairies, sun-fairies!" he called out, "Princess Crystalbelle needs your help. Take
these stones and melt them in your sun furnace. Melt them so that their colors of blue and
green and red run and mingle together. Next lay a veil of mist and cloud over the colors so
that the blue and green and red gleam through. Then this jewel will be beautiful enough for
the princess to wear in her hair on her wedding day."

This is exactly what the sun-fairies did. The three brilliant jewels, the sapphire, the
emerald and the ruby, were melted into one great gem which was more beautiful than any of
the three, and over the surface of the gem lay a veil of cloud through which the colors flashed.

This was the first opal.

The small fairy lifted the great stone in his arms. Down the mountainside he flew, across the top of the palace he skimmed and he laid the opal at the feet of Princess Crystalbelle.

The princess gazed at the magnificent jewel and she thought she had never seen anything as beautiful in the whole of her life.

"Look, there is the blue of the sea," she cried, "and I can see the deep green of the forests as well as the glowing red at the heart of a fire. And best of all, the colors are soft and misty as though gleaming through a veil of cloud."

On her wedding day, when the princess married her Prince of the Far Isles Over the Sea, she wore the great opal in her shining black hair. No princess had ever looked more beautiful than the Princess Crystalbelle on that day. The people of her land celebrated her wedding, but the fairies most of all because, together, they had found something for the princess to wear in her hair. Princess Crystalbelle treasured the opal, and all her life it remained her favorite jewel. She told her children how the opal came to be made and, in time, she gave it to her eldest daughter to wear on her own wedding day. This girl did the same with her eldest daughter, and so the opal, whose soft beauty grew with the years, passed from generation to generation. And to this day the misty beauty of the opal is often admired even more than the vivid colors of the sapphire, emerald or ruby.

THE

Stone-cutter's Wishes

JAPANESE

Many years ago, when fairies lived in forests and
meadows, and when spirits made their homes
among mountains and rivers, there lived in Japan a stone-cutter. His home was a small hut
close to a mountainside, near the great volcano Fuji-san. This mountain was also the home
of a mountain spirit who could make wishes come true.

The stone-cutter worked very hard. He spent each day, in the burning sun and in the
heavy rain, cutting huge slabs of rock which he sold to builders to use when building
houses. Sometimes he sold the rocks to sculptors. They carved statues out of his rocks and
then polished them until they gleamed. Because the stone-cutter was a skilled man, he had
many customers and he was never short of food, or clothes, or money for his tools. He was
content in his small home by the mountain, for he had everything he needed.

Then one spring day, the stone-cutter was asked to carry a large piece of rock to the
house of a rich man. This rich man had a lake in the grounds of his house and he wanted to
set up a great statue in the middle of the water. The stone-cutter, with the heavy slab of rock
on his back, trudged through the gates of the rich man's home and into his private gardens.

45

There, through an open doorway, he saw one of the rooms of the house. Many objects, more beautiful than anything he had ever seen, filled the room. On the walls hung rich tapestries and wonderful paintings in golden frames. A large bed stood in the middle of the room. Sheets made from the purest silk covered the bed and soft pillows were heaped at its head. Fine golden curtains hung round the bed.

The stone-cutter was amazed. "What a fool I am for living such a simple life," he said to himself. "My bed is the mud floor of my hut and my pillow is a bundle of cloth. I wish I were a rich, powerful man, with a bed covered with silk sheets and hung with golden curtains!"

Now, you will remember that the stone-cutter's mountain was the home of a mountain spirit who could make people's wishes come true. As soon as the stone-cutter had made his wish, he heard a voice speaking in the air around him.

"Your wish is granted!" said the mountain spirit. "May it bring you happiness!"

The stone-cutter was startled but he could see no one, so he thought he must have imagined the voice. He set down the rock he was carrying and returned to his little home. What a surprise he had when, instead of his hut, he saw a magnificent house which was filled with treasures of every kind.

"This is the life for me!" he cried joyfully, "Now I am more powerful than a stone-cutter!" He threw away his tools and for many weeks he lived idly among his riches.

Soon spring passed and it was summer-time. Each day the sun rose high in the sky, its hot rays burning the people below.

"Bring me an umbrella made of cool, blue silk!" the stone-cutter-turned-rich-man ordered his servants. "Now, hold it over my head to keep off the rays of the sun." But it was not enough to stop the sun. Its fierce rays burned down on the rich man and on the countryside around. The heat scorched the ground so that the crops turned brown and the rivers dried up.

"Why is the sun mightier than I?" wondered the stone-cutter-turned-rich-man to himself. "I wish I was the sun and more powerful than a rich man."

"Your wish is granted!" said the mountain spirit. "May it bring you happiness!"

And the stone-cutter-turned-rich-man found that he was, indeed, the mighty sun.

"This is the life for me!" he exclaimed. "Now I am more powerful than a stone-cutter and more powerful than a rich man."

For many weeks he was happy shooting his rays at the Earth. His gentle warmth made the crops grow, but sometimes he sent down such hot rays that the crops dried up and died. Then he noticed that a small cloud would sometimes come between him and the Earth, and the power of the cloud kept the burning rays from reaching the ground.

"How does the cloud, which is so tiny, prevent my rays from burning the land?" wondered the stone-cutter-turned-rich-man-turned-sun. "I wish I was a cloud and more powerful than the sun."

"Your wish is granted!" said the mountain spirit. "May it bring you happiness!"

And the stone-cutter-turned-rich-man-turned-sun found that he was, indeed, a cloud.

"This is the life for me!" he cried. "Now I am more powerful than a stone-cutter, more powerful than a rich man and more powerful than the sun!" And he was happy for a while, trapping the burning rays as he moved across the face of the sun.

The summer soon passed and in the autumn he would send down rain in rushing torrents of water which flooded the rice fields and destroyed the flimsy homes of the peasants. Only the great mountains of rock stood above the floods, unmoved by the storms.

"How can the rock be stronger than my rain?" wondered the stone-cutter-turned-rich-man-turned-sun-turned-cloud. "I wish I was a great rock so that I could be more powerful than a cloud!"

"Your wish is granted!" said the mountain spirit. "May it bring you happiness!"

And the stone-cutter-turned-rich-man-turned-sun-turned-cloud found that he was, indeed, a great rock.

"This is the life for me!" he exclaimed. "Now I am more powerful than a stone-cutter, more powerful than a rich man, more powerful than the sun and more powerful than a cloud!" For some time he was happy in his towering strength.

Then one day he felt a trembling run through him. He looked down from his lofty height and saw, far below on the ground a stone-cutter cutting out huge slabs from his mountainside.

48

"How can this be?" wondered the stone-cutter-turned-rich-man-turned-sun-turned-cloud-turned-rock. "How can a little man be mightier than a great rock? Oh, I wish I was a stone-cutter!"

"Your wish is granted!" said the mountain spirit. "May it bring you happiness!"

And the stone-cutter-turned-rich-man-turned-sun-turned-cloud-turned-rock found that he was, indeed, a stone-cutter again.

Once more he found himself beside his mountain. The magnificent house had vanished, but his little hut still stood there. Inside, he found his stone-cutter's tools safely gathered together. Now he had no great riches, he could not burn the crops nor flood the plains, nor was he as strong as a mighty rock. But he was happy to be a stone-cutter again, working hard in sun or rain. He lived contentedly for the rest of his life, grateful to the mountain spirit for teaching him that it is better to be happy with a simple life than to be rich and powerful.

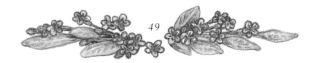

THE

Mountain of the Moon

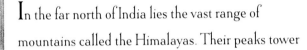

In the far north of India lies the vast range of mountains called the Himalayas. Their peaks tower into the sky and are covered with snow all year round. No humans live in these remote and silent places, but the ice fairies make their home there, living in peace in the frozen wilderness. They avoid the lower slopes of the mountains where humans live, preferring the safety of the distant peaks.

When the sky is clear and blue, some of the snow-covered mountains shine like liquid gold in the sun's rays. At dawn and sunset, they change to a rosy pink. In the evening, one of the tallest mountains often gleams with a silvery light, so this mountain is known as the Mountain of the Moon. On the side of this mountain is a cave. Long ago, two ice fairies, Soma and his wife, Surya, made their home here. Their life was happy and all day long they laughed with the wind or played with the flurries of snow falling outside their cave.

Now, all ice fairies knew that it was foolish to go too far down the mountainside, but one spring morning Soma and Surya ignored this wisdom. From their cave they could see streams which had escaped the clutch of winter and were flowing like sparkling ribbons far below.

At the sides of the streams were meadows filled with sweet spring flowers.

"Soma, let's go down to that meadow," begged Surya, gazing at the green grass and the brilliant flowers far below. "It looks so beautiful in the warm sunshine!"

Soma hesitated. He knew that it was dangerous but, like Surya, he was tempted.

"All right," he agreed. "We'll go for just a few minutes but we must not linger near the homes of human beings."

The two left their cave and skimmed down the mountainside, flying swiftly towards the distant meadow.

"Oh Soma!" cried Surya. "Can you feel the warmth of the sun? Can you smell the fragrance of those blossoms?"

In their excitement the two fairies flew through the meadow and into a wood beyond. Soma sprang into the branches of the trees.

"Shall we build a home in the tree tops?" Soma asked, and they both laughed with joy at the idea of living in this sunny land. Soon they came to the banks of a stream where they gathered wild lotus blossoms and Surya hung them around her neck in a beautiful garland.

"Look at those silver fish!" cried Surya, and they splashed about in the water, laughing and holding hands. When, at the end of the day, the sun began to set, Soma and Surya found a bank close to the stream. They sat down on the soft grass and were soon fast asleep, quite forgetting the wise rule of the ice fairies. The countryside around them was dark and the only sounds were the cries of the night creatures and the rustle of the night breeze in the leaves. Gradually the moon stole into the sky. Its light flooded across the waters of the stream and up the bank where Soma and Surya lay asleep. Then the light fell on the faces of the two sleeping fairies and woke them both.

"Surya!" cried Soma. "Look how beautiful the stream and trees look in the moonlight!"

53

"Yes," agreed Surya, "It is silvery like the light on our own Mountain of the Moon."

She rose softly to her feet. "Play me some music, please," she asked, and Soma took up the small bamboo pipe which hung round his neck and started playing a slow, gentle tune. Surya danced gracefully on the bank of the stream, singing an old Hindu song and quite forgetting the wise rule of the ice fairies.

Now it so happened that the king of Chandigarh had left his palace for a few days to hunt wild animals in the forest. With his hunting companions, he had settled for the night further down the same stream where Soma and Surya also slept. When the sound of music crept along the banks of the stream, it eventually awoke the sleeping king.

He sat up and listened. "Who can be playing that music and singing in the middle of the night?" he wondered. Quietly he rose to his feet, picked up his bow and arrows and

without disturbing his companions, he crept along the bank of the stream. Suddenly he saw in front of him a beautiful young girl, dancing and singing in the moonlight.

"There is no girl as lovely in my city of Chandigarh," he thought, "and there is no one who sings and dances as beautifully as this girl."

He did not know that Surya was an ice fairy and he immediately fell in love with her. Then he noticed Soma sitting on the bank playing his pipe. At once, the king decided to shoot the young man so that he could have Surya for himself. He raised his bow and, taking careful aim, he sent an arrow flying straight to Soma, striking him and causing a dreadful wound.

Surya, delighting in her own song, had not heard a sound. Then she realized that the music from the pipe had stopped. She turned towards Soma and gave a cry of alarm. Her husband was lying on the ground, his face deathly pale in the moonlight and a red wound gaping in his chest. Surya threw herself on the ground beside him, calling his name – but in vain. Soma lay motionless as if already dead.

"Now I will show myself to the girl," thought the king, and he rose from his hiding place among the bushes. Surya heard the rustle of the leaves and sprang to her feet in fear.

"Do not be afraid!" said the king. "I will not harm you. Come with me to my palace and live there with everything that your heart desires. You shall have garments woven from the most delicate fabrics. You shall have the rarest and finest foods in the whole of India. You shall have servants to obey your every command."

Now Surya was very afraid but she raised her head and looked at the king. "There is only one thing that I desire," she replied, "and that is my husband, Soma. We are ice fairies who live on the upper slopes of the Mountain of the Moon. Our ways are not the ways of humans and I will never live with you in your great palace. What you have done is a wicked and cruel thing. Now go! Return to the land of the humans and leave us to our wild mountain ways!"

When the king heard this, he was ashamed. Slowly he turned away and went back to

his hunting companions. Because he was ashamed, he shouted at the sleeping men and made them pack up the tents at once. They all hurried away from the stream and the forest, back to their own city.

Meanwhile Surya knelt by Soma's side and placed her hand upon his heart just below the cruel wound. To her great joy, she felt a fluttering under her fingers!

"Soma is still alive!" she thought joyfully. "Now I must appeal to the gods of the Mountain and ask for their help to make him well."

Surya turned her face towards the Mountain of the Moon and begged the gods to let her husband live.

"We were foolish to ignore the wise rule of the ice fairies," she admitted humbly. "Please forgive us! Please hear my prayer! For your power is stronger than the wickedness of a human!"

At last Surya's desperate plea reached the throne of the great god Indra. He decided that Surya and Soma had suffered enough and that he would help them. Disguising himself as a Brahmin, or holy man, he approached the bank where Soma lay weak and helpless. Surya wept at his side. Indra held a small glass dish in his hand and, bending down, he sprinkled a few drops of liquid over Soma.

Color flooded back into Soma's cheeks immediately and, at the same time, the terrible wound shrank and disappeared as though it had never been. Soma raised himself from the ground and then sprang to his feet. When Surya saw Soma standing before her, full of life as before, she fell on her knees before Indra.

"Oh great god, you have chosen to help us. For this we will always be truly grateful," she cried.

Indra looked at the two ice fairies. "You were foolish to ignore the wise rule of the ice fairies," he said sternly. "Now return to your own haunts where you are safe." Then the great god rose to his throne among the other gods, and Surya and Soma were once more alone on the bank of the stream.

"Come Surya," said Soma, and took her hand. "We have been fortunate this time and

the gods have been good to us. Let us return to our own slopes on the Mountain of the Moon. There is the home of our own people where we can live in safety and happiness."

So away the two flew. They left behind the sparkling streams, the dense forests and the sunny flower-strewn meadows and returned to their snowy slopes. Here they settled once more in their cave, happy and grateful to be among their own people. Never again, even when the spring came and covered trees with blossom, did they leave the Mountain of the Moon. They had learned that the paths of man and the paths of the fairies are different, and that they do not always meet in happiness.

THE

Golden Spear

IRISH

Once upon a time, in a beautiful part of Ireland
called Erin of the Streams, there lived a famous
king called Connla. He had fought many battles and won victories over his enemies. Now
he lived in peace, ruling wisely over his contented people. Nearby lived the king's sister,
Nora. She was a brave and gracious lady who was married to one of Erin's greatest
warriors. With her lived a little old woman who was Connla and Nora's mother. The little
mother and her son and daughter had known great hardships in the past. They would often
meet to talk together about the old days, when they had been a simple family living in a
little house at the foot of a great mountain.

When Connla and Nora were children they had lived alone with their mother in a
poor peat cottage. In front of the cottage was a meadow, and beyond, the towering
mountain face. Most of the mountain was covered with heather, but near the top the
rocks showed sharp and bare where the summit rose into the sky like a spear. At sunset,
the rays of the setting sun would strike this barren mountaintop, turning it a gleaming
gold. The two children named it the Golden Spear.

59

All summer long the children played in the meadow and woods nearby. They climbed through the heather and explored the mountain stream. In the winter they sat by the fireside with their mother. They ate the fresh bread which she baked, drank the milk from their own cow and listened to their mother's stories. The three of them were as happy and contented as anyone in the world.

One summer's day when the sun blazed down on the meadow, Connla and Nora were resting from the heat in the shadow of a hawthorn bush. By chance they saw a thrush cowering in the grass nearby. It looked too frightened to move.

"Nora, Nora!" cried Connla, "Look at that thrush, and see, up there in the sky! That great hawk is going to grab the thrush!"

Nora saw that she had only a moment in which to act. At once, Nora sprang to her feet. She clapped her hands and shouted at the hovering hawk. Startled by the sudden noise, the bird swerved away, up into the sky.

The thrush rose happily into the air and perched in the hawthorn bush by the children. Sitting there, it burst into the most beautiful, trilling song. The children listened in amazement to the beauty of the sound.

"Oh, Connla!" said Nora, "Have you ever heard such beautiful music before?"

"No," answered her brother, "I don't think there has ever been more beautiful music."

To their surprise, the thrush then stopped singing and spoke to the children.

"Thank you both for saving my life," it said. "I am singing to thank you because Connla saw that I was in danger and because Nora frightened away the hawk. But if you want to hear music even more beautiful, watch the bare mountaintop at evening time until it is turned to gold by the setting sun. At that moment, where the heather ends and the barren rocks begin, you will see nine little pipers come out, and the music they play is sweeter than mine." With that, the thrush flew away and the children went home to wait for the evening.

When the sun started to set, Connla and Nora sat outside their home, watching the mountain. As the great bare peak turned into shining gold, they both saw a little door in the

side of the mountain suddenly open. Now, they knew the mountain very well and yet they had never seen this secret door before. Through the door trooped nine little pipers. Each was dressed in green and gold, and as they marched, one behind the other, through the heather, they played their pipes. The music was so sweet that even the birds, who were already in their nests, came out to listen. The nine little pipers marched down the mountainside and disappeared into the woods nearby.

"The thrush was right," said Connla, "That music was the sweetest in all the world."

The next day the children went to play in the woods and the stream at the side of their meadow. The sun glinted through the leaves of the overhanging trees and the stream sparkled and flashed in the sunlight.

"Connla, Connla!" said Nora. "Have you ever seen anything quite so sparkling and brilliant before?"

"No," answered her brother, "I don't think I have ever seen anything quite so beautiful."

"That's because you have not seen the crystal hall of the fairies beyond the mountain," piped a voice above the children's heads. And there, perched on a branch nearby, was the thrush whose life they had saved.

"If you want to see the crystal hall, all you have to do is follow the nine little pipers when they march down the mountainside at sunset," said the thrush, and it flew away into the woods.

That evening, Connla and Nora waited for the sun to sink. They sat on the doorstep of their little house and watched eagerly. Slowly the shadows spread across the meadow and up the side of the mountain until the bare top was gleaming like gold. In a moment, the hidden door swung open and the nine little pipers trooped out and down the mountainside. Connla and Nora quickly followed them as they passed through the heather and into the woods, the pipers playing their music all the time. At last they marched out of the wood and towards another mountain peak which also gleamed in the sunlight like a golden spear. The children saw a door, like the one in their own mountain, open up, and the nine little pipers marched in. Connla and Nora followed close behind.

As the children passed through the door, it closed behind them and they found themselves walking on clouds of gold and amber, and purple and red.

"Oh, Connla," cried Nora in amazement, "we are walking in the sunset!"

Soon they came to a gap in the clouds and they saw a ladder leading down from the sky. The nine little pipers disappeared down the ladder and Connla and Nora hurried after them. The sweet music of the nine little pipers wafted up the ladder towards the children, and as they followed the pipers down, they heard another sound mixing with the music.

Soon they realized that it was the sound of waves. When they reached the

bottom of the ladder, they found themselves on the edge of the sea.

Standing on the shore, Connla and Nora saw the nine little pipers walking along the golden path which stretched over the waves from the shore to the setting sun. They walked as safely as they had walked through the heather.

"Oh, Connla!" cried Nora, "I wish we could follow them!"

As she spoke those words, Connla gave a shout and pointed across the waves. Galloping towards them was a white horse with a flowing mane and golden hooves. On the horse's back sat a little man dressed in green and gold.

"If you want to follow the nine little pipers, Nora, climb up in front of me," he ordered. "Connla, you must perch behind."

When the children were safely seated, the little man cried out "Swish!" and away over the tips of the waves galloped the white horse, with its mane flowing in the air and its hooves gleaming gold on the waves.

After a little while, the man cried out, "Hold on tightly!" and in that moment, the horse started to sink through the waves, down, down, through the soft cool waters of the sea until its feet rested on the golden sand at the bottom. Just ahead of them, the children saw the nine little pipers disappearing through a gap in a cluster of dark rocks.

"Now you must go on your own!" said the little man, and as soon as the children had scrambled off the horse's back, he cried out, "Swish!" and the horse and rider both rose up through the water and vanished.

Connla and Nora hurried to the rocks where the nine little pipers had disappeared and pushed through the gap. To their astonishment, they found themselves in a beautiful sunlit meadow. A stream wound through the grass and flowers, and the children followed it. They walked through the meadow to a garden of roses, and beyond this garden stood a snow-white palace. Huge silver doors, studded with jewels, stood open at the palace's entrance. The children walked through these doors and they stopped and stared in amazement at the scene in front of them. Their eyes were dazzled by the brilliance of the light which shone in the crystal hall. The walls and the floor and the ceiling were all made of crystal which sparkled and flashed like a thousand diamonds. Great crystal pillars supported the roof and silver brocade, sewn with pearls, hung on the walls. At the end, on a crystal throne sat the Fairy Queen. The nine little pipers marched down the great glistening hall. They marched past couches made from mother of pearl, where hundreds of fairies dressed in clothes of

gossamer were seated. The nine little pipers bowed to the Fairy Queen and stood at the side
of the throne.

The Fairy Queen, who was lovelier than the Evening Star, rose from her throne and
glided towards the children. She took Connla by her right hand and Nora by her left, and
sat them on each side of the throne. Then she lightly clapped her hands and the nine little
pipers started playing their pipes once again. The fairies in the hall rose and danced over the
crystal floor like leaves wafting on a breeze.

Connla and Nora listened to the music and watched the graceful fairies, but soon they
found their eyelids growing heavier and heavier and before they knew what was happening,
they had fallen into a deep sleep.

The next morning they awoke and found themselves lying in beds of silk. But something
extraordinary had happened. Connla had grown into a tall, handsome young man and Nora
was now a lovely young woman.

"Oh Nora, how you have grown!" cried Connla.

"Not as tall as you, Connla," answered Nora, and she ran to hug her brother just as the
Fairy Queen entered the room.

"How did we grow so tall in one night?" they asked her in amazement.

The Fairy Queen laughed like a crystal bell. "It is more than one night," she said. "Why,
you have both been asleep for seven years."

"But what of our mother?" exclaimed Connla and Nora together.

"She is safe and well and she knows of your adventures," the Fairy Queen replied.
"Today you must return to her, but before you go, I will give you these presents." First, she
gently placed a necklace over Nora's head. "This necklace is made from the ocean spray and
the sparkle of sunshine. Keep it safe. Many adventures lie ahead of you. You will face them
with courage and you will be the mother of many fearless sons and daughters," she told her.

Then she turned to Connla. "Your destiny, Connla, is to be a king in Erin of the Streams.
You will have to face many battles to win your crown, but these presents will help you." She
then laid a cloak around his shoulders and fastened it with a golden brooch. "When your
time comes for battle," she explained, "always fasten your cloak with this brooch. It will
protect you and bring you victory." She then gave Connla a helmet, a shield and a spear.

"Go, now, home to your little mother," she said. And the two young people, carrying their magic gifts, walked out of the fairy palace, back through the rose garden and meadow, following the stream as they had before, until they found themselves once more under the sea. Again, a little man dressed in green and gold and riding a white horse with a flowing mane and hooves of gold, pulled up beside them.

"Nora, climb up in front of me and Connla, you must perch behind," he said. When they were safely seated, the little man called out, "Swish!" and the horse rose through the water and across the tips of the waves to the sea shore. There, instead of telling them to get down off the horse, the little man cried out, "Close your eyes!"

With their eyes shut, Connla and Nora could hear the sound of the horse's hooves galloping across a meadow. "You can open your eyes now," said the little man.

Connla and Nora could hardly believe their eyes. In front of them was their own sweet meadow but instead of their little house, a fine mansion stood in its place. The horse came to a stop and they both dismounted. "Swish!" cried the little man and he and the horse disappeared into the sky.

The front door of the fine house opened and Connla and Nora's mother came running out. She threw her arms round their necks and kissed and hugged them over and over again.

"Oh, Connla! Oh, Nora! Welcome home!" she cried. "How fine and strong you have both grown. I knew you were safe but I was lonely without you."

That night the three of them sat in their own home in front of the fire and Connla and Nora told their mother of all their adventures. They told her how the Fairy Queen had said that Connla would one day have to fight great battles and would be a king in Erin of the Streams. Then they told how Nora would be tested with many trials and bear many children. In time, all these things came to pass, but that evening, long ago, the three of them were as happy as it was possible to be, talking of the past and thinking, with joy, of what the future held for them all.

How the Fairies Came

ALGONQUIN

Once, long ago when only the Algonquin people roamed the wooded shores of the great Ottawa River in Canada, there lived ten sisters. Each sister was more beautiful than any other girl in the land, but the youngest sister, whose name was Swan Feather, was the loveliest of all.

Because of their great beauty, many strong and handsome braves would visit the girls' home to woo them. They would offer gifts of deerskin moccasins adorned with porcupine quills and delicate trinkets carved from shell and horn. The nine oldest girls preferred the most handsome of the men. One by one, these nine girls were married and went to live with their husbands' families, until only Swan Feather was left. Swan Feather, who was wiser than her sisters, had many suitors but refused them all, preferring to remain in her family home.

One day an old man came to visit Swan Feather. Nobody knew where he had come from. His body was bent and feeble, and he carried no gifts with him. However, Swan Feather saw that his eyes were bright and heard that his voice was strong.

"My name is Osseo," he told Swan Feather. "Will you be my bride and come with me to live in my home beyond the forest?"

Swan Feather looked into his eyes and saw his innermost thoughts. There was something very special about him.

"Yes," she agreed, "I will."

The day for the wedding was fixed and Swan Feather's nine older sisters and their handsome husbands were invited to the wedding feast. They all came eagerly, curious to see who Swan Feather had chosen as her husband. But when they arrived, they looked with scorn on Osseo and jeered at their sister for marrying such an old man.

"Why," they exclaimed, "your husband is older than our grandfather! He is bent like a gnarled tree. He hasn't offered you gifts as our husbands did. What kind of home will he have for you? You'll not find happiness with him!"

Swan Feather smiled patiently and answered quietly, "Wait and see."

When the wedding celebrations were over, Osseo took Swan Feather's hand. "Come with me," he said. "My home lies many miles from here, beyond the great forest."

Osseo and Swan Feather started their journey back to Osseo's distant home, and the nine sisters with their husbands walked with them along the forest paths. After a short distance, they came upon a mighty tree which, many years before, had been struck by lightning and now had a great gaping hollow in its trunk.

"Wait!" commanded Osseo, and he limped towards the tree and went inside its hollow trunk. Within seconds he appeared again, but now he was a tall, upright young man with a proud walk and a noble bearing. The sisters and their husbands were astonished and the sisters looked at Swan Feather with envy, because Osseo was more handsome than their own husbands. But Swan Feather just smiled gently. Osseo once more took her hand and led the party through the forest. After many miles they came to a fine wigwam in a forest clearing.

"Is this to be our home?" asked Swan Feather and again all her sisters looked at her with envy.

"No," replied Osseo, "but we will rest here for a little while and refresh ourselves."

When they had all entered the large interior, they found a banquet spread before them. Delicacies of every kind were displayed in bowls and platters. "The food you see is magic and if you eat it, you will receive a gift," said Osseo, and they all sat down to enjoy the feast.

"I wonder when we shall get our gifts and what mine will be?" the eldest of the sisters remarked to her husband. "I should like a carved mirror made from polished stone."

"I would prefer a large drinking cup carved from a single antler," replied her husband. And all the nine sisters and their husbands whispered among themselves, each hoping that their gift would be the finest of all.

Suddenly they felt the wigwam quake and start to rise from the ground. Up and up through the still evening air it rose and, as it did so, their surroundings changed. The banquet vanished, golden wires took the place of the walls and the birch-bark mats on which they sat

were turned into perches. The sisters and their husbands jumped up in alarm, but before
they could cry out they suddenly found they had been transformed into birds. Some of them
were indigo buntings with vivid blue wings; others were robins with scarlet breast feathers;
others still were brilliant yellow warblers with flashing tails. They all began to hop about the
cage and their voices changed, so that instead of speaking ugly words, they now sang
beautiful songs. This was the gift that Osseo had promised them.

Alone among the sisters, Swan Feather was not transformed into a singing bird. Her gift was that her loveliness grew even greater. Her hair gleamed like the lake waters and shone like one of the brightest evening stars. She stood quietly beside Osseo and was unafraid. At last the cage reached the far-off land above the treetops and beyond the stars where Osseo lived.

"Now we have reached our journey's end," he said, and stepping from the cage, he helped his bride climb out. Swan Feather found herself near a grand lodge. Osseo led her through the entrance and she saw her new home for the first time. The birdcage, filled with the nine sisters and their husbands, was hung outside the entrance.

"One day, your sisters and their husbands will be sorry for their unkindness and their greed and will gain their freedom," Osseo explained. "Then we will all be together in harmony. But until that day comes you must trust me. Do not bring the cage into our home and never open the door of the cage."

Swan Feather, who had a kind heart, felt sad for her imprisoned sisters and their husbands but she knew Osseo would keep his promise, and that one day all would be well. She and Osseo lived in great happiness in their far-off land. In time a son was born to them. The boy was as upright and as noble as his father and he shone as brightly as his mother. He learned from Swan Feather's gentle manner to be loving and from Osseo's bravery to be a warrior. When the boy grew old enough, Osseo made him a little bow and a set of arrows so that he could learn to hunt as did all the people in his band. One day, the boy looked around for something to shoot at in order to practice his shooting skills. Nearby hung the birdcage filled with the rainbow-colored singing birds.

Although he had been warned many times never to touch the birds or their cage, he now forgot what he had been told.

"I'll shoot my arrows at the birds," he thought. Without thinking, he opened the door of the cage and let out the birds. At that instant the cage broke from its fastening and started to fall gently towards Earth. The boy and the many-colored singing birds also found themselves floating down and down and down. From the entrance of her home, Swan Feather saw her son spinning gently towards the far-away land.

"Osseo!" she cried out in despair.

At once Osseo ran to her. When he saw what had happened, he took Swan Feather's hand and together they leaped after the falling boy. The cage, the singing birds, Osseo, Swan Feather and their son all spun and twirled gently towards the distant Earth. The cage was the first to land and it came to rest in the middle of a lake. Immediately the cage was changed into a little green island covered with soft grasses and moss. Osseo, Swan Feather and their son, together with the singing birds, floated gently through the air and onto the island.

"Now the time has come, as I said it would, for us to live together in harmony," explained Osseo. As soon as he had spoken, everyone felt a change come over them. Their bodies grew light and airy and gossamer wings grew from their shoulders. The gaily colored birds with their beautiful singing voices, together with Osseo, Swan Feather and their son, were turned into the first fairy spirits. So Osseo's promise was fulfilled and they lived together happily on their little green island and the waters around it.

Even to this day, on summer nights when the stars glitter in the sky, some children from the nearby villages say they can hear the distant singing voices of the fairies who were once singing birds. Other children who are even more fortunate, say they glimpse the fairies dancing and playing on the green island. These children always claim that among the fairies there are two who are more radiant than all the others, and who seem to be the king and queen among the group. Although nobody can ever be certain, the people living around the lake think that these two fairies are Osseo and Swan Feather who now live forever in the peace of their little island.

Fairy Flora

The fairies care for all growing things. There are a number of flowers and trees that the fairies particularly love; they are a special feature of the art in this book. The following notes describe some of the folklore surrounding these 'fairy flora':

Bluebell
CONSTANCY & KINDNESS

Bluebells are also known as wood hyacinths, and as Cuckoo's Boots, Crowtoes and Endymion (after the woodland lover of Diana, the goddess of hunting). The Scottish name for the plant is Deadmen's Bells, for to hear the ring of a bluebell is to hear one's death knell. Fairies are summoned to their midnight revels by the ringing of these tiny flowers, which are reputed to be the most potent of all fairy flora. Legend has it that children who venture into bluebell glades will be held captive, while adults will be pixie-led, until met by another mortal and guided out.

Clover
THOUGHTFULNESS

Because fairies do not like to be seen by humans, they disappear in the blink of an eye, but some people believe that a four-leafed clover may prevent this and allow a mortal to see fairies in their invisible state. A four-leafed clover is famous for bringing luck and it gives a person the power to break fairy spells and see through their magic.

Cowslip
GRACE AND PENSIVENESS

Cowslips are an invaluable fairy flower, for their blossoms provide shelter from the rain. Above tufts of wrinkled oval leaves, their tall stems sway with parasol-like clusters of fragrant, buttery yellow flowers, each one painted with five tiny red dots ("rubies, faerie favours," according to Shakespeare). In England they are known as the Culver's Keys, for their heads resemble a bunch of keys and these are said to hold the power to unlock the way to fairy treasure. The cowslip appears in "The Fairies' Jewels" to reflect the characteristics of Princess Crystalbelle.

Forget-Me-Not
LOVE & DEVOTION

Fairy flowers may be divided into those that belong to them and those that give protection from them. Forget-me-nots are one of the latter group and like the cowslip have the power to unlock secret treasures, often supposed to be guarded by fairies or spirits. The delicate forget-me-not has long been the emblem of love and remembrance. The forget-me-not appears in "The Magic Fountain" to symbolize the devotion between Sylvain and Jocosa when they are separated.

Foxglove
INSINCERITY

Foxgloves are universally reputed to be fairy plants and it is unlucky to pick them or bring them into your home, but you will please the fairy folk if you grow the tall foxglove in your garden. The flower derives its name from Little Folks-glove, since it's believed that the florets are worn by fairies, sometimes as bonnets, sometimes as gloves. The flower has many strange folk names, such as Fairy Weed, Dead Men's Bellows, Bloody Man's Fingers and Witch's Thimble. The poison in the plant causes drunkenness and frenzy. But in Irish belief, the juice of ten foxglove leaves will cure a fairy-struck child. This juice is also an ingredient used by witches in the potion that helps them to fly. The little flecks on the flowers are said to be the fairies' fingerprints.

Hawthorn
HOPE

Like all thorn trees, the hawthorn is a sacred meeting place for fairies. It also has a reputation for being both sacred and unlucky. Among its many folk names are Whitehorn and May Blossom and its red fruit has been called Pixie Pears, Cuckoo's Beads and Fairy Thorn. Some country people in Europe still associate hawthorn flowers with the smell of the Black Death. It may be for this reason, or because of other more ancient memories, that May Blossom is still considered unlucky to bring into the home. However, the hawthorn's powerful constituents have been used by herbalists for centuries as a cardiac tonic. The Druids also used these properties to strengthen the body in old age and their smiths used the wood to make the hottest fire-wood known. Many Native Americans, like those in "The Star Maiden," used the fruit of the hawthorn to make a winter cake. They also used its long, sharp spines as probes, awls and fish hooks.

Hazel
RECONCILIATION & PEACE

From the earliest times trees have been believed to be the homes of spirits, but some trees are more sacred than others. One of the most magical is the hazel, held by the Druids to be the tree of wisdom and knowledge, poetry and fire, beauty and fecundity. A forked hazel twig is used for water divining, and some believe that it can also find gold. The hazel can offer protection from danger — a cap of hazel leaves and twigs ensures good luck and safety at sea, while a sprig of hazel will protect against lightning. According to ancient lore, the nuts from the hazel were dropped into the water to feed the sacred salmon of the Celts and these fish were then considered to be full of mystical knowledge. In England, the hazelnut has long been associated with fertility — a bag of nuts bestowed upon a bride will ensure a fruitful marriage! The hazel appears in "How the Fairies Came" to echo the theme of peace and reconciliation in this story.

Heather
GOOD FORTUNE & SOLITUDE

Heather appears in "The Golden Spear," representing the good fortune that is bestowed upon Connla and Nora. Heather thrives on wide open windy moors, and so it has also become the

78

symbol of solitude. Fairies who enjoy living undisturbed are said to feast on its stalks. Legend has it that a gift of white heather brings luck to both the giver and the receiver, whereas red heather is said to have been colored by heathens killed in battle by Christians. In ancient times the Danes brewed a powerful beer made from heather. And for centuries the heather flowers have also been a special beverage to the bee, who in return creates delightful heather honey!

Jasmine
AFFECTION & ELEGANCE
The jasmine is a symbol of beauty in China and a sacred plant of India and Persia — Hindus call it the Moonlight of the Grove, and it appears in "The Mountain of the Moon." The white jasmine is also sometimes known as the Star of Divine Hope and is associated with the purity of the Virgin Mary in Christianity. While the white jasmine is believed to symbolize deep affection, the yellow represents grace and elegance. According to folklore, to dream of jasmine means that a romance is blossoming.

Pansy
JOY AND REMEMBRANCE
Legend has it that Cupid brought color to the pansy with one of his arrows, and this flower is widely associated with love and the healing of an aching heart. The best-loved wild flowers accrue the most folk names and the pansy is certainly one of these! In addition to their most popular pseudonym of Heartsease, pansies have also been called Love-in-Idleness, Three Faces in a Hood, Tickle my Fancy, and Jack Behind the Garden Gate, as well as being the notorious, mischievous Leap up and Kiss Me. Bold-faced and multicolored, they flower blithely from spring to snowfall and are used by the fairies as a love potion. Like heather, the pansy appears in "The Golden Spear," for its meaning of joy reflects the spirit of this tale.

Peach Blossom
IMMORTALITY
The peach tree, also called the Tree of the Fairy Fruit, is presumed to have originated in China. It appears in "The Herb Fairy" because the heroine of this tale, Chun Tao, is named after its

blossom. Peaches are the symbol of immortality in China because the peach tree of the gods, which grew in the mythical gardens of Hsi Wang Mu, the Royal Lady of the West, was said to bloom only once in 3000 years, yielding the ripened fruits of eternal life.

Primrose
YOUTHFULNESS & PROMISE
Primroses make the invisible visible and to eat them is said to be a sure way to see the fairies. According to folklore, you should count the number you first see each springtime, and if there are thirteen or more, you will be lucky all year. If a nosegay holds less than thirteen, it must be protected by violets, or it is risky to take into church, or even into a house. If you lay a little posy upon your doorstep, fairies will cross your threshold as you sleep, to bless your home. In Ireland primroses are scattered before the house door to ward off the fairies, who are not supposed to be able to pass them, while in Germany, the primrose is said to open hidden treasure boxes. Some believe that the way to fairyland can be opened by touching a fairy rock with the proper number of primroses in a posy — but the wrong number opens the door to doom! The Japanese primrose appears in "The Stone-cutter's Wishes."

Rowan
PRUDENCE
If a rowan tree should take root in your garden, then your home and all who live there will be blessed, for the garden is under the special protection of the fairies, guarded against witchcraft and bad luck. For this reason the tree was traditionally planted around houses and in lonely places to deter evil spirits. The Celts believed that no witches or evil spirits could cross a door over which a branch of rowan had been nailed. In some legends, the rowan has also been called the whispering tree because it has secrets to tell to those who will listen. The fruit and the bark of the rowan have medicinal powers—there are many old remedies made from this tree. In Scotland, fires made from rowan wood were used to protect the cattle against evil fairy spirits, and it was believed that a "bewitched" horse could always be controlled by a rowan whip. Like the hazel, the rowan appears in "The Star Maiden," for the Algonquins had many uses for this plant.

Silver Birch
PATIENCE
The silver birch is an emblem of everlasting summer that prevails in the spirit world. It is also the symbol of the festival of the first fruits known as Lammas-tide, when the goodness of Mother Earth is celebrated. May Day, Whitsuntide and Midsummer are also important days, for wearing a sprig of birch in your buttonhole will work as a love charm. And in winter, the stark beauty of the birch symbolizes the serenity of nature dormant and sleeping. Folklore says that garlands of silver birch by the front door keep demons away, but the spirit of the tree can inflict madness and death. The Native Americans used the bark of the silver birch to make the legendary birch-bark canoes, hence the name Canoe Birch. They also used strips of white birch to make their wigwams, which appear in "The Star Maiden," as well as baskets, mattresses and even writing paper.

Toadstool
MAGIC & TEMPTATION
Countless folk tales and songs link fairies with toadstools whose sudden appearance and rapid growth have always intrigued people — seemingly caused by some inexplicable, supernatural force. Their unearthly shapes and colors (sometimes quite luminous) and their often hallucinogenic properties are thought to be a sure sign that they are the creation of fairies! The Fairy Ring Mushroom is the one which grows in a circular formation, marking the boundary of the fairies' favorite dancing places. The enchanting timbre of the fairies' music and revelry can lure mortal passers-by inexorably into the ring for what may seem like minutes but is actually years, sometimes even forever!

White Lotus
PURITY
The white lotus flower was sacred in ancient Egypt, India, China and Tibet and is still regarded as a symbol of purity in those countries. In medieval Germany, peasants believed that lotus flowers were nymphs in disguise and ladies would carry the flower in their hand to counteract the effects of love potions. Illustrations of the lotus appear in "The Herb Fairy."

Sources

The Magic Fountain
Adapted from the Comte de Caylus's story, "Sylvain and Jocosa," as it appeared in *The Green Fairy Book*,
by Andrew Lang, (Longmans, Green & Co., London, 1892).

The Star Maiden
Adapted from the version in *American Indian Fairy Tales*, by Margaret Compton, (Dodd, Mead & Company, New York, 1934);
and from a retelling of "The Star and the Lily" in *The Traditional History and Characteristic Sketches of the Ojibwa Nation*,
by George Copway, Chief of the Ojibwa Nation (Charles Gilpin Publishers, London, 1850).

The Herb Fairy
Adapted from the retelling in *Fairy Tales of the World*, published by Artia, Prague, The Czech Republic, 1985. Copyright © 1985 Artia.

The Fairies' Jewels
Adapted from "The Making of the Opal" in *Fairies I Have Met*, by Maud Margaret Stawell, (Hodder & Stoughton, London, 1910).

The Stone-cutter's Wishes
Adapted from "The Stone-cutter," retold in *The Crimson Fairy Book*, by Andrew Lang, (Longmans, Green & Co., 1892).

The Mountain of the Moon
Adapted from a retelling in *Hindu Fairy Tales*, by Florence Griswold, (George G. Harrap & Co. Ltd, London, 1919).

The Golden Spear
Adapted from a retelling in *Irish Fairy Tales* by Edmund Leary, (W. B. Yeats, Unwin Hyman Ltd, London, 1892).

How the Fairies Came
Adapted from a retelling in *The Red Indian Fairy Book* by Francis Jenkins Allcott, (Mifflin & Co. Ltd, London, 1917).

Fairy Flora
The information in this section was compiled with reference to the following:
Cicely Mary Barker, *Flower Fairies: The Meaning of Flowers*
K. M. Briggs, *The Fairies in Tradition and Literature*
Brian Fround & Alan Lee, *Faeries*
Claire Nahmad, *Garden Spells: The Magic of Herbs, Trees and Flowers*
Rhoda Nottridge, *A Bouquet of Flowers: Book of Days*
Helena Paterson, *The Celtic Lunar Zodiac*
Eugene Stiles, *A Small Book of Fairies*